GAME ON!

BLUR ON THE BASE PATHS

BY BRANDON TERRELL

www.12StoryLibrary.com

Copyright © 2015 by Peterson Publishing Company, North Mankato, MN 56003. All rights reserved. No part of this book may be reproduced or utilized in any form or by any means without written permission from the publisher.

12-Story Library is an imprint of Peterson Publishing Company and Press Room Editions.

Produced for 12-Story Library by Red Line Editorial

Photographs ©: iStockphoto, cover

Cover Design: Emily Love

ISBN
978-1-63235-044-2 (hardcover)
978-1-63235-104-3 (paperback)
978-1-62143-085-8 (hosted ebook)

Library of Congress Control Number: 2014937412

Printed in the United States of America
Mankato, MN
June, 2014

TABLE OF CONTENTS

CHAPTER 1

RACING FOR HOME

Bottom of the seventh inning. Down by one run. Two outs. And Ben Mason was stepping up to the plate.

It's now or never, he thought.

Ben's teammates cheered him on from the dugout. The loudest shouts came from his best friends, Logan, Gabe, and Annie. They played for the East Grover Lake Grizzlies.

Because Ben had a quick glove and a strong arm, he manned third base. What he didn't have, though, was speed. He hoped his new cleats, a pair of Fusion Speeds he'd gotten for his birthday, would change that.

Ben tapped the shiny new cleats with his bat and let out a deep breath.

"Come on, Ben! You can do it!" Coach Parrish shouted. Their coach was actually Logan's dad. During games, they all made sure to call him Coach Parrish.

On the mound, the pitcher for the Newton Lizards stood hunched and staring at the catcher. He was trying to intimidate Ben, but he was failing miserably. Ben had already gotten two hits in the game, and he was planning on smacking a third.

Ben stepped into the batter's box and raised his bat.

The Lizards' pitcher threw a fastball. Ben watched as it popped into the catcher's mitt.

"Strike one!" the ump shouted.

Ben wasn't fazed. He rarely swung at the first pitch.

He twisted his hands on the bat's grip and got ready for the next pitch.

It was a curveball that hung high in the strike zone. He swung and connected.

Crack!

Ben's hit sliced between the first and second basemen. He ran to first, rounding the base as the ball bounced into right field.

"Take two," the first base coach yelled.

Ben dug in, tearing toward second as the outfielder threw the ball in. Most players would have easily gotten a stand-up double, but Ben barely reached base before the throw.

Phew! That was close, he thought. He needed more speed from his Fusions.

The dugout went wild. His friends whistled loudly.

The first base coach was Gabe's dad, Coach Santiago. He clapped and shouted, "Nice one, Ben! Two outs. Run as soon as the ball is hit."

Ben nodded.

The team's first baseman, a lanky kid named Tyler Murphy, stepped up to the plate. Ty was so tall and thin he looked like a daddy longlegs spider when he ran. All he needed to do was get a base hit, and Ben was sure to score the tying run.

Ty fouled off the first pitch, sending the ball up over the backstop and into the stands, where their parents sat watching the game. Many wore the Grizzlies' team colors, brown and red.

The pitcher tried to get Ty to swing at two changeups out of the zone. Ty wouldn't bite. The count was now two balls and one strike.

Next, the Lizards' pitcher threw a fastball down the pipe, and Ty jumped on it.

Crack!

The ball sailed over the pitcher's head, and right over Ben's, too. As it bounced into the center field grass, Ben ran hard toward third.

The Grizzlies' third base coach, Coach Johnson, waved him around and excitedly shouted, "Go! Go! Go!"

Ben lowered his head, rounded third, and broke for home.

He was going to score!

Suddenly, the spikes on his left cleat stuck in the dirt, and his new shoe split open at the heel. It was as if Ben had a flat tire. He stumbled forward and nearly fell.

Out of the corner of his eye, Ben saw the Lizards' second baseman catch the relay from the outfield and throw the ball home. He hobbled toward the plate. It was going to be close.

Ben dove, sliding headfirst into home as the Lizards' catcher received the throw. He swiped his massive mitt across Ben's hands before they reached the plate.

"You're out!" the umpire roared.

Disappointed sighs rose from the crowd. Ben lay on the ground, not wanting to get up.

He wished he could just disappear with the dust cloud.

"That's game," the umpire said. "Lizards win, 4-3."

CHAPTER 2

FLAT TIRE

"I can't believe my new cleats," Ben said after the game. "The shoe just tore as I was heading home."

Ben sat on the wooden bench in the dugout and inspected his red and black Fusion Speeds. They were a popular new cleat, so new that Ben was the only Grizzlies player to own them. The heel of his left shoe had split open, making it appear as though it had a mouth.

Logan must have thought the same thing. He snatched it out of Ben's hand, moved the two pieces of the shoe up and down, and said in a croaking voice, "I need a mint. My breath smells like feet."

"Give me that." Ben grabbed the torn shoe back and put it in his equipment bag. "It's not funny. I don't know how I'm going to play the rest of the season."

Nearly everyone else had already packed up their things and left with their parents. Ben's parents were both at work, so thankfully they didn't see his epic failure at the game today. His bike was locked up at a nearby rack alongside Annie's. She lived across the street from him, and they biked almost everywhere together.

Now the only people left in the dugout were Ben and his friends. Logan's and Gabe's dads were standing together by the bleachers and chitchatting about the game.

"Didn't you just get those?" Logan asked.

"Yeah," Ben mumbled.

"Bummer," Gabe said, shaking his head. "That's gotta be bad luck or something."

Gabe was *super*-superstitious. He'd worn the same pair of socks to every game for the past two years—without washing them. They used to be white. Now, thanks to the infield dirt and his catcher's equipment, they were a mix of gray and brown. Ben figured it wasn't just good luck. The smell of those things probably made batters' eyes water so much they couldn't see the pitches coming in.

Logan shrugged. "So get your mom to exchange them for a new pair. No big whoop."

"She can't," Ben said. "When she bought them, the guy at Mega-Sports told her the Speeds are so popular they've been back-ordered, for like months."

The Speeds were really expensive, too. Before Ben's parents had even considered buying them for him, Ben had promised he'd take special care of the cleats and do extra chores to help pay for them.

"Oh," Logan said. "Bummer."

"I know where we can get you a new pair of cleats," Annie suggested with a smile.

Ben knew what she was going to say. "You want to go to Sal's, don't you?" he asked.

"Yeah!" she said.

Sal's was a used sporting goods store in downtown Grover Lake. Its owner, Sal Horton, always seemed to know exactly what somebody was looking for. Ben had never bought anything at Sal's before. He liked his equipment new, not all scuffed up and worn out.

"Sal's isn't going to have a pair of Fusion Speeds," Logan said. "Heck, Sal probably would think they're rocket-propelled shoes."

Annie shrugged. "I bet he'll have something, though," she said. "Probably something even better."

Logan snorted back laughter. "Better than Speeds?"

"You never know," she said.

Ben didn't really have a choice. Maybe Sal's would have something to hold him over until he earned enough money to buy a new pair of cleats, or until Mega-Sports was able to replace his torn Speeds.

"Okay," Ben said. "Why not?"

CHAPTER 3

A TRIP TO SAL'S

Most everything on the east side of Grover Lake was old and historic. The town's main street was lined with brick and stone buildings. There was a barbershop, a bank, and a couple of small restaurants. One of these places, the Lake Diner, served the best milk shakes in town. Ben and his friends had conducted extensive research to come to this conclusion.

Sal's Used Sporting Goods was located near the Lake Diner. It had a giant, frayed orange awning, and a picture window with the store's name written in white block letters across it.

Ben and Annie skidded to a stop. Gabe, who'd been riding on the back pegs of Ben's bike, hopped off. Logan did the same from his spot behind Annie.

The bell above the door jingled as they walked inside. Sal's was cluttered and cramped. Everywhere, tall shelves overflowed with sporting equipment.

"Evening, gang!" a booming voice echoed through the store. Sal was a large, barrel-chested man with wispy combed-over hair and a gray beard. He stood behind a glass counter. The counter displayed a number of special items. There were signed baseballs and footballs, and even a few rare baseball cards.

"Hey, Sal!" Annie said excitedly.

"Big game today?" Sal asked. "How did you do?"

"We lost," Logan answered.

"Oh, I'm sorry to hear that," Sal said.

Annie jerked a thumb in Ben's direction. "Ben's cleat ripped when he was trying to score the tying run," she said.

"Yeah, he's a real speed demon," Logan joked.

Ben punched him in the arm.

"Ah, I see." Sal crossed his arms over his massive chest and thought for a moment. "Looking for something to give you an extra spring in your step, are you, Ben? I think I may have just the thing for you. Follow me."

Sal wove his way through the labyrinth of shelves, humming "Take Me Out to the Ball Game." Ben and his friends followed. They ended up at a wall of baseball gloves, bats, and helmets. Shelves of dusty, old cleats lined the bottom of the wall.

"Thanks, Sal," Ben said. "I'll take a look and see if something fits."

Sal wagged a meaty finger at him. "Not so fast," he said. "There's one particular pair of cleats I have in mind. I think you'll find they're *just* right for you."

"Like Cinderella's glass slipper," Logan said with a smirk.

Ben elbowed him in the side.

"They wouldn't happen to be a pair of Fusion Speeds, would they, Sal?" Gabe asked.

"A Fusion *what*?" Sal asked, his face scrunched up in confusion.

Logan said, "See. Told ya."

Sal lowered himself to one knee and began rummaging through a mound of old shoes. Ben took a second to poke around and marvel at his surroundings. Even though it looked like a tornado had blown through the store, everything in Sal's was in its correct department. There were shelves of football helmets and pads. A soccer display with a metal cage of balls. An area devoted to basketball gear, and a wall of exercise equipment and weights. It all had a thin layer of dust on it, as if the place hadn't been cleaned since it opened. Ben wasn't entirely certain when that was, but he was pretty sure Sal's had been in business since his parents were his age.

"A-ha!" Sal exclaimed. "Here they are."

With great effort, the shop owner rose to his feet. In his hands were a pair of worn shoes. He held them up proudly, and Ben's heart dropped.

They were the oldest, dustiest pair of baseball cleats he'd ever seen.

CHAPTER 4

A LESSON IN BASE STEALING

The grin on Sal's face stretched from ear to ear. "Well," he said. "What do you think?"

What do I think?! Ben thought.

The cleats Sal held in front of Ben's nose were the opposite of his Fusion Speeds. They may have been white and green once, but time and use had turned them a faded shade of gray. The laces were frayed; one was broken and half-missing. Ben glanced at Logan. His cheeks were turning red from trying to hold back laughter.

"They're . . . um . . . nice," Ben said.

He could tell that Sal wasn't buying his fake sincerity. "Ben, do you know who Rickey Henderson is?" he asked.

"I do!" Annie piped in. She even raised her hand, as if they were in school.

"Yeah, I've heard of him," Ben said. He knew Henderson had played baseball, but he couldn't remember exactly what position he played or why he was famous.

"Well, this particular pair of cleats once belonged to him," Sal explained.

"Whoa. Those are Rickey Henderson's old shoes?" *Okay*, Ben thought, *that's actually pretty cool.*

He picked up the gray shoes and examined them more closely. Inside, on the tongues, the number 24 had been scribbled in black marker.

Sal began to lumber back toward the counter. "You see," he said as he walked, "Rickey Henderson played in the majors during the 1980s and '90s for a number of teams, but mostly for the Oakland Athletics. He holds the record for the most stolen bases in baseball history, and he's the only American League player to ever steal more than a hundred bases in one season. He did that three times."

"That's amazing," Gabe said.

"In fact," Sal said, "they used to call Rickey 'The Man of Steal.'"

"Cool," Logan said under his breath. Even he was impressed. "I want an awesome nickname like that someday."

"Speedy base runners have always been an important part of baseball," Sal continued. "You've all heard of Ty Cobb, correct?"

"Didn't he play like over a hundred years ago?" Annie said.

"That's right." Sal unlocked the display counter, reached in, and took out a baseball card in a plastic case. The card featured a man wearing a gray uniform with a D on the chest, for the Detroit Tigers. "A 1909 Ty Cobb baseball card. One of my prized possessions."

"Whoa," Ben whispered. Sal placed the card on the counter, and the foursome crowded around to stare at it.

"You see," Sal explained, "Ty Cobb set the record for most single-season stolen bases *waayyy* back in 1915, when he stole 96 bases. His record went unbroken for nearly fifty years."

Ben couldn't believe it. "That card must be worth *thousands* of dollars."

Sal continued. "He also stole home more than any other player. Fifty-four times, to be exact." He placed the card back in the display case, and then leaned both elbows on the glass. He looked down at the pair of cleats, then back up at Ben. "Well, what do you say, Ben? Would you like this particular pair of cleats?"

"Yeah, sure," Ben said with a shrug of his shoulders. It was cool that the cleats had a history to them, even if they weren't Fusion Speeds. They would do for now.

Ben pulled a few crumpled bills from his sock and laid them on the counter next to the cleats.

"I'll take them," he said.

CHAPTER 5

TEST RUN

The Grizzlies' next game was a few days later. They were playing a team from the neighboring town of Rockville, the Earthquakes. The game took place on one of the two baseball diamonds located on the outskirts of Grover Park, a large park in the center of town. A row of towering elm trees along the third base line cast the field in late afternoon shadow.

Ben and Annie biked to the game together. Once again, Ben's parents were working late and weren't able to make it. Ben had the cleats he'd bought at Sal's tucked in his backpack. He hadn't tried them out yet.

As he sat on the bench tying his left cleat, Gabe walked over and asked, "You ready to break them in?"

"From the looks of it, they're already broken," Logan joked.

Ben finished tying the pair of new white laces he'd bought. The cleats were rigid from all the years they'd sat on Sal's shelf, and there was still a bit of dust on them. Ben quickly rubbed it off with his palm.

He stood and stretched his legs. The cleats creaked as he walked.

"How do they feel?" Annie asked.

"Uncomfortable," Ben answered. "I have no idea how I'm going to run in them."

"Maybe they'll loosen up as we play," Gabe suggested.

Ben took a few tentative steps around the dugout. Maybe he was crazy, but it *did* seem like the cleats were becoming more flexible, like they were shedding years of stiffness and disuse with every step.

The Grizzlies batted first. Ben was third in the lineup, so he snagged a helmet and bat and waited his turn. Logan, batting leadoff, hit a single.

The next batter swung at a pitch low and outside. He hit a dribbling grounder that the second baseman had to run in to field. Logan made it safely to second, but the batter was thrown out at first.

Ben looked down at his cleats and tapped them gently with his bat.

"All right," he whispered, "let's see what you've got."

He stepped into the batter's box.

The first pitch was high, and Ben's bat never left his shoulder.

The second pitch was right down the heart of the plate. It was just what he was waiting for.

Ben swung and connected solidly.

Crack!

The ball soared into left-center field, found the gap between the outfielders, and skipped toward the fence.

Like a bolt of lightning, Ben took off toward first. He made a wide turn toward second and could feel his feet moving faster than ever. He stomped on second just as the Earthquakes' center fielder scooped up the ball and tossed it in. Ahead of him, Logan was trotting safely home to score the game's first run.

Ben raced on to third as the cutoff throw came in. He hit the dirt, sliding hard. He was moving too fast. He slid right past the base.

"Quick!" shouted the stunned third base coach. "Back on the bag!"

Ben scrambled to his knees and reached out with one hand. He heard the *thwapp* of the ball striking the third baseman's glove. The Earthquakes' player swiped at Ben, but he got his hand on the bag just in time.

Whoa! That's never happened before, he thought. *I overran the base.*

The Earthquakes' starting pitcher stared him down as he led off the base. Then the pitcher wound up and delivered to the next batter, Ty. The ball was in the dirt. It skipped under the catcher's mitt, toward the backstop.

"Go!" the third base coach shouted.

Ben broke for home, digging in with his cleats and pumping his arms and legs. The Earthquakes' pitcher raced him to the plate, holding out his glove to receive the throw from the catcher.

Ben slid safely under the tag.

"Way to go, Ben!" shouted Gabe.

"That was awesome!" Annie added.

"Dude," Logan said, clapping Ben on the back as he entered the dugout. "I've never seen you run that fast."

For the entire game, Ben moved like he never had before. When an Earthquakes' batter hit a looping pop fly into shallow left—a ball that would almost certainly land for a base hit—Ben dashed after it, dove, and caught it. The next time he made it to first base, he stole second.

And then third!

By the time they hit the fifth inning, the Grizzlies were cruising toward an easy victory.

The final score was Grizzlies 7, Earthquakes 1.

CHAPTER 6

A RUN-IN

"Okay, let's try this," Annie said after the game.

Ben and his friends were the only players remaining on the field. Annie held up a black plastic stopwatch and swung it around one of her fingers by its strap.

"We're timing your speed, Ben. Come on. Take first." She walked across the field to second base.

Ben, still sporting the cleats he got from Sal's, stepped on first.

Annie held out her stopwatch. "From a dead stop, it takes the average major leaguer about 4.4 seconds to get from first to second."

"How does she know that?" Gabe asked under his breath.

"That's for a *major leaguer*, Annie," Logan said. "We're thirteen."

"Duh. I don't expect Ben to run faster than Mike Trout," Annie said. "Six seconds is probably our best speed. Maybe more for Ben. No offense."

Ben shrugged. "None taken."

"Okay. Are you ready?" she asked.

Ben just nodded. He lined up like a track runner, one leg out in front, the other positioned on the edge of the base.

"On your mark . . . get set . . . *go!*"

Annie thumbed the stopwatch, and Ben broke toward second. He lowered his head, pumped his arms, and felt his feet flying under him.

As his foot *thumped* on second base, Annie held up the stopwatch. There was a look of awe on her face. "Five-point-three seconds," she said.

"Holy cow!" Logan exclaimed. "I don't believe it!"

Ben didn't either. Whatever uncertainty he had about his new cleats had been completely washed away. He couldn't wait to wear them in the game against the Fighting Hornets from West Grover Lake.

As if on cue, a group of kids walked up to stand on the other side of the chain-link backstop. Ben recognized the guy in the lead: Jacob Fuller. Jacob played for the West Grover Lake baseball team. He was tall and muscular, and even though he was the same age as Ben and his friends, he looked like he was in high school.

"Nice game out there," he said. To most, it was a simple compliment. Jacob's words, however, dripped with loathing.

"Thanks, man," Logan said, trying to be cool. He was still wearing his mitt. He slapped his fist loudly into it.

"Gonna need to play better than that, though, if you're gonna beat us on Friday," Jacob said. His two friends, one of whom Ben thought was named Micah something, snickered.

"Come on, guys," Annie said, "let's get going."

Ben grabbed his cleats from the bench, and the quartet left the dugout. However, as they passed Jacob and his pals, the tall bully saw Ben's shoes and asked, "What do we have here?" He quickly seized the cleats before Ben could pull them away.

"Hey!" Ben shouted. "Give them back!"

Jacob laughed. "Where did you get these smelly old things? Your great-grandpa?"

Ben lunged at Jacob and tried to grab the cleats. Jacob easily dodged him.

"Here, let me do you a favor," Jacob said as he tied the laces of Ben's cleats together.

He wound up and threw them as high as he could into the air. The cleats sailed in a wide arc, twisting and turning, landing directly in one of the tall elm trees along the third base line. Their laces wrapped around one of the branches, and they hung there, stuck.

"What did you do that for?!" Logan shouted. He walked up to Jacob and shoved him in the chest.

Logan had no fear. Ben, on the other hand, didn't like confrontations. So he bit his lip and tried to stay calm, even though his cheeks burned crimson with a combination of embarrassment and anger.

"Let's get out of here," Ben said, pulling on Logan's arm.

Jacob laughed. "Yeah. Run away," he said. "We'll see you Friday!"

"Man, I can't stand that kid," Logan muttered under his breath as they walked away.

Ben agreed, but said nothing.

Then he and his friends gathered their things, climbed on their bikes, and pedaled away from Grover Park without looking back.

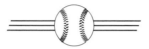

Ben waited until after sunset before sneaking out of the house and returning to the field at Grover Park. He wanted to make sure Jacob and his friends were gone. He didn't want to have another run-in with them.

The park was cloaked in hazy darkness, with pockets of lamplight scattered throughout. He leaned his bike against the backstop and craned his neck upward. Ben knew which tree Jacob had chucked his shoes into, but he had a hard time locating them in the dark.

There they are, he thought.

The cleats dangled from a branch about thirty feet up. Ben searched out the tree's lowest branch, jumped up, grabbing it with both hands, and began to climb.

The going was tough. He pulled himself onto the first branch, until his stomach rested on it. He swung one leg over. A small twig snapped off, its splintered remains scratching his arm and digging into his skin.

"Ouch!" Ben cried. In the eerily quiet park, his voice sounded extra loud.

He stood on the thick branch, which creaked under his weight. As he reached up for the next branch, he lost his footing. Ben scrambled to stop from falling, wrapping his arms around the tree's trunk and hugging it tight.

"That was close," he whispered.

After catching his breath, Ben looked up at the cleats. He thought about reaching for the next branch again . . . and hesitated.

"Are they really worth falling out of a tree and cracking your head open?" he asked himself aloud.

With a shake of his head, he answered his own question.

Ben sat down on the branch, swung his legs out, and dropped safely to the ground. Maybe he was better off without the shoes. Sure, it seemed like they made him run faster. Possibly. But he'd been beyond humiliated when Jacob and his friends laughed at the beat-up cleats.

Besides, it's not like he'd thrown out his old pair of cleats, the ones he wore before his mom bought him the Fusions. They were small, but they'd work.

I'll just wear those instead, he thought.

Ben gave the cleats one last look.

"Sorry, Sal," he said under his breath.

Then he hopped back on his bike and rode home, empty-handed.

CHAPTER 7

A BAD FIX

"What do you have there?" Annie asked.

It was the next afternoon, and Annie was just getting to practice. Her equipment bag, bulging with baseballs and bats, hung from the front of her bike. A Grizzlies cap was crammed low on her head, and her pigtails stuck out from it like they were trying to escape.

Her question had to do with the cleats Ben was pulling from his bag. They were black with yellow streaks along the sides.

"Uh, my cleats," Ben said as he crammed his foot into the old shoe. He'd spent about an hour searching for them the night before. He'd found them at the bottom of a cardboard box in the garage labeled *DONATIONS* in his mom's handwriting.

"Hey, Ben!" Logan shouted from the infield. He and some of the other guys were already out on the field. "Want to toss the ball around and warm up?" He lobbed a baseball into the air and caught it behind his back.

"Sure!" Ben hurriedly put on his cleats. As he stood, he winced in pain. They were really tight. He could feel his toes crammed against the sides, and it hurt to walk.

Annie stared at him, confused. "You in pain?" she asked.

Ben tried to hide his agony with a smile. "No. Not at all. Totally cool."

"Why didn't you just go after the cleats you bought at Sal's?" Annie asked. "You *do* know how to climb a tree, right?"

"Yeah." He decided not to tell her that he actually *tried* to climb the tree.

"Are you afraid of heights or something?"

"I'm more afraid of *falling* from heights. But no."

"Then why'd you just leave them up there?" she asked.

Ben shrugged. "Dunno."

But he did know the real reason. Because if he wore those old cleats at the game against West Grover Lake, and Jacob Fuller saw him, he'd get nothing but grief.

He would rather not have to deal with that distraction again.

"Any day, Mason!" Logan called out. He was lying in the grass, pretending to nap, using his glove as a pillow.

"Coming!" Ben stood up and took a few steps in his old, small cleats. They felt pretty brutal. They would probably give him huge blisters by the time practice was over.

After the team warmed up, Logan's dad sent them to their usual positions on the field. Ben stood at third, smacking his fist into his glove. Annie took her position over at second, Logan in right.

"Okay," Coach Parrish said, wielding a bat. "Let's field some grounders. Ben, you're up!" Gabe, standing beside Coach at home, tossed him a ball. Coach lobbed it up, swung the bat, and sent a grounder down the line.

It was a simple play, but because of his too-small cleats, Ben stumbled and fell. The ball sailed past his outstretched glove and into left field.

Ben banged his glove against the dirt in frustration.

The rest of practice went about the same way. Every time Ben had to make a play, he was hesitant. Unsure. Scared to move. And though he tried to act like everything was normal, he couldn't stop thinking about his cleats. How they hurt his feet. He used to attack the ball. Now, he was being cautious, afraid he'd twist an ankle or something.

It was the worst practice Ben had ever had, and by the time it was done, he just wanted to go home and plop down in front of the TV and forget entirely about baseball and the next day's game against West Grover Lake.

That was, if he could pry the tiny cleats from his throbbing feet.

CHAPTER 8

REUNITED

Friday's game was played at a field near East Grover Lake High School. Because the east siders wanted to keep up with the fancy new field over at West Grover Lake High, their field had new dugouts, rows upon rows of metal bleachers, and an electronic scoreboard with the Grizzlies' mascot in the middle of it.

Ben's parents were both able to make it to this important game. Both proudly sported Grizzlies' hats and shirts.

For the first time ever, though, Ben was actually dreading playing baseball.

He was one of the last players to reach the field. Many of his teammates were already playing catch along the third base line, near their dugout. On the other side of the field, wearing yellow and blue, was the West Grover Lake team, the Fighting Hornets. The tall, imposing Jacob Fuller stuck out like a sore thumb.

"Afternoon, Ben," Coach Parrish said as Ben stepped into the dugout. He had a score book in his hands and was finalizing the lineup. "Ready to have a great game?"

"You bet, Coach." Ben prayed his coach couldn't tell how he was *really* feeling.

Ben sat down next to Gabe on the bench. As he was about to change out of his street sneakers, Annie arrived.

"Ben!" she said. "Think fast!"

She quickly tossed something at Ben, and he snagged it out of the air before it hit him in the face.

It was his pair of used cleats from Sal's.

He was stunned. "Wait, did you . . . ?"

". . . scurry up a tree like a squirrel this morning before school and retrieve your shoes because you were too afraid of being made fun of by Jacob Fuller and his gang of *un*-lovable misfits?" Annie finished with a smile. "Yep."

"I don't know what to say. Um, thanks."

"Of course," she said. "You know, it wasn't these silly old shoes that made you fast. I mean, they're just shoes. I doubt they were really even Rickey Henderson's. But they did make you more confident."

"Hey! It's the 'Return of the Cleats!'"
Logan jogged over to the dugout and joined
the three friends.

"What are you waiting for, *amigo*?" Gabe
asked, punching Ben lightly in the shoulder.
"Put them on and let's go win us a ball game."

That sounded good to Ben. Forget what
Jacob Fuller thought. These cleats were his,
and they were going to help him have the
best game of his life.

Ben slid the shoes on and laced them up.

When he took the field for warm-ups,
he caught Jacob Fuller looking at him. One of
Fuller's cronies, Micah, chuckled and pointed
at Ben's shoes.

Jacob shook his head and asked, "Hey,
didn't I throw those out for you?"

Ben ignored him.

After a short warm-up, the umpire shouted two words that gave Ben goose bumps every time he heard them: "Play ball!"

CHAPTER 9

THE BIG GAME

Since the Grizzlies were the home team, they took the field first. Their pitcher was a boy named Andy Otto. Andy threw fast, but he had some problems with accuracy. As catcher, Gabe did his best to help him out from behind the plate.

"Batter up!" The ump's voice carried across the whole ballpark. The crowd cheered, and the first Hornet batter stepped up to the plate.

Andy's fastball was thankfully on target. He mowed down the Hornets easily, striking out the first three batters.

When the Hornets took the field in the bottom of the first, Jacob Fuller walked confidently up to the mound. He was their team's ace pitcher, so Ben wasn't surprised to see him starting. He toed the rubber, taking his time as he threw a few warm-up pitches.

Coach Parrish rattled off the lineup. Ben was batting third, his usual spot. Logan hit leadoff, Annie was fifth, and Gabe was batting seventh.

"Get it started, Logan!" Ben shouted.

Logan stepped up to plate. He watched the first couple of pitches from Jacob. One ball and one strike. On the third pitch, he hit a solid single down the third base line.

Crack!

Jacob wasn't rattled, though. He struck out the next batter on three consecutive pitches.

Ben adjusted his helmet, knocked the dirt off his cleats with his bat, and stepped into the batter's box. Jacob leaned forward, looked down his nose, and smirked. His first pitch sizzled high and tight. Ben barely had time to jump back before it whizzed past his head.

"Hey!" Annie yelled from the dugout. "He did that on purpose!"

Coach Parrish shushed her. "Calm down, Annie."

Ben's hands started to shake. He tried not to be rattled, but it was hard—a baseball going as fast as a car on the interstate had nearly taken his head off.

Jacob's second pitch was in the dirt. Two balls, no strikes. The next pitch was right where Ben thought it would be—down the middle. He leaned forward and swung.

Crack!

The ball bounced past Jacob and into center field. Logan hurried from first to third. Ben made it safely to first.

As Ty stepped up to the plate, Ben crept off first and thought of Rickey Henderson, The Man of Steal, confidently running around the bases.

He looked across to the third base coach, who tapped his belt buckle. That was the "steal" sign.

Jacob, pitching from the stretch, went into his windup.

Ben broke for second.

He dug his cleats into the dirt and ran as hard as he could. By time the catcher had popped up and whipped off his mask, Ben was already standing on the base.

"Great steal, Ben!" Coach Parrish said.

Jacob Fuller glared at Ben, who just smiled and tipped his helmet.

Ty hit a looping pop fly into shallow right field, and the Hornet players couldn't come up with it. Logan scored easily, and Ben dashed around from second to home in no time.

At the end of the first inning, the Grizzlies were up 2-0.

Andy pitched a strong game, only allowing a handful of Hornet hits. Jacob Fuller got two singles and a double, but he was left stranded every time. The last time he reached third base but failed to score. He jogged back to the dugout and threw his helmet to the dirt in frustration.

He took out his annoyances on the mound. Jacob practically shut down the Grizzlies. The only time they made it on base was when Gabe, who was not normally a power hitter, crushed a solo home run in the fourth inning. As he touched home plate, he pointed down to his legs and said, "The lucky socks worked their magic again!" Ben thought about how long it had been since Gabe's mom had washed those dirty old lucky charms, and he wrinkled his nose in disgust.

The Grizzlies' defense was spectacular. When one of the Hornets hit a deep drive to right field, Logan raced back, leaped into the air, and snagged it before it could go over the fence. The crowd roared.

"Amazing catch, Logan!" Ben shouted.

Once, with a Hornet on first, Annie dove for a ground ball heading up the middle, scurried to touch second, and then fired over to Ty for a double play.

Heading into the top of the seventh and final inning, the Grizzlies had a 3-0 lead and were rolling toward a shutout against the Hornets.

And that was when it all fell apart.

Andy walked the leadoff Hornet on four straight pitches. The next batter chased after a high pitch and flied out to left field, leaving the runner at first. The following batter slapped a single past a diving Annie. As the next batter stepped up to the plate, Ben hoped and prayed he would hit into a double play.

Standing in the on-deck circle was Jacob Fuller, the Hornets' best hitter. Ben knew he'd be tough to get out.

"You got this guy, Andy," Ben said.

Andy's first pitch, though, was just what the Hornet hitter was looking for, and he connected solidly with it.

Crack!

The ball sailed between the left and center fielders, bouncing all the way to the wall. By the time it was tossed in, one run had scored, and the remaining base runners stood at second and third base.

The score was 3-1. There was one out. And Jacob Fuller was stepping up to the plate.

This could be trouble, Ben thought.

Ben's heartbeat quickened. He dug his cleats into the dirt and crouched into position.

Jacob watched the first pitch smack into Gabe's mitt for a strike. The second was low and inside. The third was in the dirt, and Gabe had to drop down to keep it from skirting past him.

On the fourth pitch, Jacob Fuller swung.

Crack!

Ben didn't even have to watch. The way the ball left the bat, it was clear that he'd knocked the stitching off it. He'd be surprised if the ball didn't land somewhere in the next county.

The Hornets leaped off the bench and crowded around home. When Jacob trotted around and stepped on the plate, they surrounded him and jumped up and down in celebration.

After Jacob's home run, Coach Parrish pulled Andy from the game. He left with slumped shoulders, mumbling, "Sorry, guys," as he headed toward the dugout. His relief, a short sidearm pitcher named Travis, quickly got the last two outs of the inning.

The Grizzlies had started the seventh up by three runs.

They'd ended it down by one.

CHAPTER 10

GOING FOR IT

Bottom of the seventh. Down by one run. One out. And Ben was coming up to bat. It was now or never.

Again, he thought.

Logan had led off the Grizzlies' half of the seventh inning with a double. The following batter had struck out looking.

Ben tapped his cleats with his bat and hoped they had as much magic in them as Gabe's lucky socks.

Jacob Fuller was still on the mound for the Hornets, and his fastball still had a lot of sizzle. His first pitch was right down the center of the plate. Ben swung and missed.

"Strike one!" shouted the ump.

Ben stepped out of the box and looked over at the dugout. His teammates were all standing at the chain-link fence that protected the dugout from foul balls.

"You can do it, Ben!" Annie shouted.

Ben stepped back into the box. The pitch was high, but Ben mistakenly chased after it. He connected, hitting a dribbling ground ball down the third base line. It was an ugly hit, but it caught the Hornets' third baseman completely by surprise.

"Run it out!" Coach Parrish shouted.

Ben tore down the line, sprinting as fast as he could. The third baseman fielded the ball with his bare hand and threw it across the field.

Ben's foot hit the bag milliseconds before the first baseman caught the throw.

The umpire waved Ben safe.

Logan was now standing on third base.

"Nice wheels!" Gabe shouted from the dugout.

Jacob Fuller grumbled and kicked angrily at the dirt around the mound. As Ty stepped up, the Hornets' pitcher glared over his shoulder. Ben shuffled off first base, and Jacob quickly threw the ball over. Ben dove back safely.

Then Jacob threw a fastball to Ty, who hit a lazy fly ball to shallow center. It was an easy play for the Hornets outfield. Logan and Ben could not advance.

The Grizzlies were down to their last out.

Annie stepped into the batter's box. There was fire in her eyes.

With the game on the line, Jacob Fuller's first pitch, a fastball, looked like it came out of his hand in slow motion. Ben watched as it sped toward home, could practically see the stitching as it rotated. Annie's eyes never left the ball. She swung the bat around.

Crack!

The ball sailed into the outfield. Ben was so caught up by the hit he just stood there for a moment and watched as the ball found a gap between center and right field, heading toward the fence. He forgot there were two outs and that he should have been running at the crack of the bat.

"Ben! Run!" Gabe's dad hollered from his position as first base coach.

Ben took off like a bolt. He could feel his cleats propelling him forward, digging into the infield dirt, making him faster with each step.

He didn't stop at second. Ben rounded the base and chugged on toward third. Ahead of him, Logan was already nearing home. The Grizzles were going to tie the game for sure.

But Ben didn't want to tie. He didn't want extra innings.

He wanted to win.

When he was almost to third, Ben looked up at the third base coach, who was waving his arm, sending him home.

"Go! Go!" he shouted.

Ben sped down the third base line like a blur. This wasn't going to be like last time. No, these cleats weren't going to rip. He wasn't going to stumble. He wasn't going to be called out.

Not again.

Ben looked down at home. The catcher crouched over the plate, waiting for the ball. Behind him, an angry Jacob Fuller backed him up. The relay throw came in from the right fielder. The second baseman snagged it out of the air, turned, and fired the ball home.

Ben dove, sliding headfirst into the plate.

Thwack!

The ball struck the catcher's mitt.

Dust erupted all around them.

Ben's fingers grazed home plate as the catcher swiped his glove at him.

Time seemed to stand still as everyone waited for the call.

"*SAFE!*" the umpire bellowed.

Ben leaped to his feet as the Grizzlies' bench cleared. Gabe picked him up in a massive bear hug, while others slapped high fives.

"Wow!" Annie shouted as she squeezed past teammates to reach Gabe and Ben. "I didn't think you'd beat that throw!"

"Forget Fusion Speeds!" Logan added as he joined them. "I want a pair of those bad boys!"

Ben couldn't believe it. They'd beaten Jacob Fuller and the Fighting Hornets.

The Grizzlies shook hands with the Hornets. Even Jacob Fuller mumbled "Good game" as Ben bumped fists with him.

Then Coach Parrish announced, "Tonight's milk shakes at Lake Diner are on me! Great game, Grizzlies!"

The team quickly cleared their things from the dugout. Ben switched into his sneakers, tying the laces of his cleats together.

His parents were waiting for him near the bleachers. When Ben looked at his mom, she clapped. His dad walked over and gave him a high five.

"Great job, Ben," his dad said. "That was something amazing."

Before Ben could say anything, his mom eyed his cleats. Her brow furrowed. "What an interesting pair of shoes," she said. "Those aren't the ones we got you for your birthday. Where did you get them?"

"Well," Ben said, "it's . . . um . . . kind of a long story."

"How about you tell it to us over milk shakes?" his dad asked, ruffling Ben's hat and hair.

"Sure thing."

"Okay. Meet us at the car," his dad said.

Ben waited for his friends, who were loading up their equipment bags.

Logan was still breaking down the game play by play. "And then, oh man, I can't believe Ben just dove like that . . ."

He raised his arms over his head like Superman and mimicked Ben's slide into home.

"Faster than The Man of Steal, *amigo*," Gabe said.

Ben grabbed his bag and slung his cleats over one shoulder. Then the four friends headed off to celebrate their big win.

THE END

ABOUT THE AUTHOR

Brandon Terrell is a Saint Paul-based writer. He is the author of numerous children's books, including picture books, chapter books, and graphic novels. When not hunched over his laptop, Brandon enjoys watching movies and television, reading, baseball, and spending every spare moment with his wife and their two children.

ABOUT THE BASEBALL STARS

Ty Cobb was one of the first players voted into the Baseball Hall of Fame in 1936.

Nickname: The Georgia Peach

Years in the Majors: 24, from 1905 to 1928

Teams: Tigers, Athletics (Philadelphia)

Position: Center field

Record: Career Batting Average (.366)

Rickey Henderson was voted into the Baseball Hall of Fame in 2009.

Nickname: The Man of Steal

Years in the Majors: 25, from 1979 to 2003

Teams: Athletics, Yankees, Padres, Mets, Red Sox, Dodgers, Angels, Mariners, Blue Jays

Position: Left field

Records: Career Steals (1,406), Career Runs Scored (2295)

Mike Trout won rookie of the year in 2012, his first full year in the majors.

Nickname: Millville Meteor

Years in the Majors: from 2011 to present

Team: Angels

Position: Center field

THINK ABOUT IT

1. Imagine you were in Ben's shoes. What would you think about the old cleats Sal picks out? Would you even try them out? Would you do anything differently when Jacob tosses them into a tree?

2. Motivation is what drives characters to make choices and do the things they do in a story. What is Ben's motivation throughout the story? Use examples to explain your answer.

3. Read another Game On! story. In *Blur on the Base Paths*, Ben is the main character. What role does he play in the other book? Does he act differently or the same? Use examples from both books to explain your answers.

WRITE ABOUT IT

1. Sal tells Ben and his friends about Rickey Henderson and Ty Cobb, two of his heroes. Do you have any heroes you look up to? Describe them. Write about what they do and explain why you admire them.

2. Imagine you were playing baseball on the Grizzlies' team. Think about the position you would play. Where would you be in the batting order? Then write a story in which you are playing a game with Ben, Gabe, Logan, and Annie.

3. At the beginning of the story, Ben fails to score the tying run and his team loses. Have you ever been in a similar position when you were unable to do something? Write about it. What happened? Why didn't you succeed? Did that make you try harder next time?

GET YOUR GAME ON!

Read more about Ben and his friends as they get their game on.

Break to the Goal
Logan is worried about trying out for the Grizzlies soccer team, so he heads down to Sal's Used Sporting Goods. He picks up a new soccer ball and learns about another player who struggled at first, David Beckham. Can Logan get his game on before his teammates turn against him?

Dive for the Goal Line
Gabe Santiago is a backup running back. On the day that he loses his lucky football gloves, the team's starting running back, Ben Mason, gets hurt. Now Gabe needs to get his game on as he is thrust into the starting running back role.

Drive to the Hoop
Annie Roger will do anything to prove that girls can play basketball just as good as boys. She heads over to Sal's Used Sporting Goods and learns all about Nancy Lieberman, a women's basketball legend. Can her newfound inspiration carry Annie and her friends to the championship?

READ MORE FROM 12-STORY LIBRARY

Every 12-Story Library book is available in many formats, including Amazon Kindle and Apple iBooks. For more information, visit your device's store or 12StoryLibrary.com.